If Everybody Did

IF EVERYBODY

DID

written and illustrated
by
JO ANN STOVER

journeyforth
Greenville, South Carolina

If Everybody Did

Written and Illustrated by Jo Ann Stover

©1960 Jo Ann Stover; David McKay Company, Inc., New York

©1989 BJU Press

Greenville, South Carolina 29609

JourneyForth Books is a division of BJU Press.

Printed in the United States of America

ISBN 978-0-89084-487-8

35   34   33   32   31   30   29   28   27   26   25   24

When there's only one, that's just SOMEBODY. . . .

But when there's one... and one... and one.... and more.......
that's EVERYBODY.

Did you ever think of
what would happen if
EVERYBODY did
things like............

Make tracks?

This is what would happen if Everybody did

Spill tacks ?

this is what would happen if Everybody did

Pull off a bud?

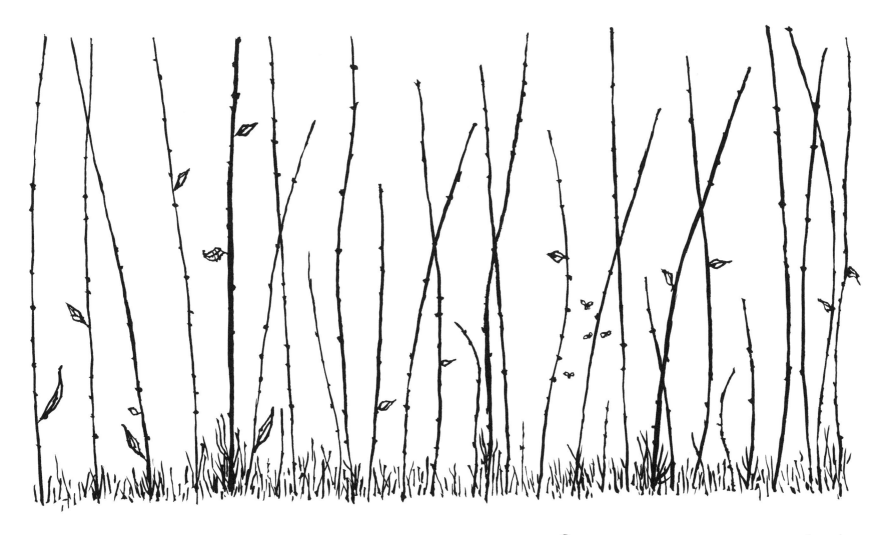

this is what would happen if Everybody did

Jump in the mud?

this is what would happen if Everybody did

SLAM THE DOOR ?

THIS IS WHAT WOULD HAPPEN IF EVERYBODY DID

STOMP AND ROAR ?

THIS IS WHAT WOULD HAPPEN IF EVERYBODY DID

SQUEEZE THE CAT?

THIS IS WHAT WOULD HAPPEN IF EVERYBODY DID

Forget your hat ?

this is what would happen if EVERYBODY did

Step on Daddy's feet ?

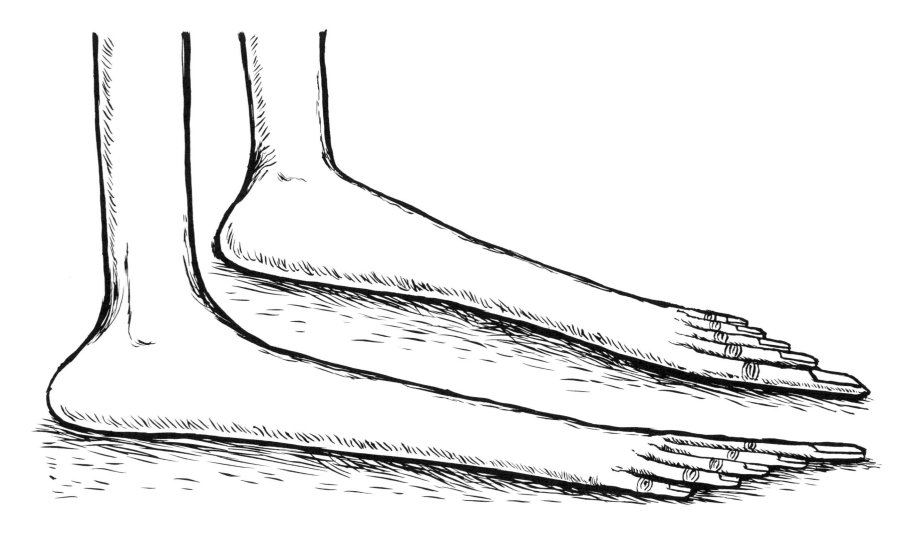

THIS IS WHAT WOULD HAPPEN IF EVERYBODY DID

keep changing your seat?

tish is awht uldwo paphen if yeverbdyo idd

Make a smudge?

This is what would happen if Everybody did

Eat all the fudge?

THIS IS WHAT WOULD HAPPEN IF EVERYBODY DID

MAKE A BIG SPLASH?

Mash hash?

This is what would happen if Everybody did

Climb too high ?

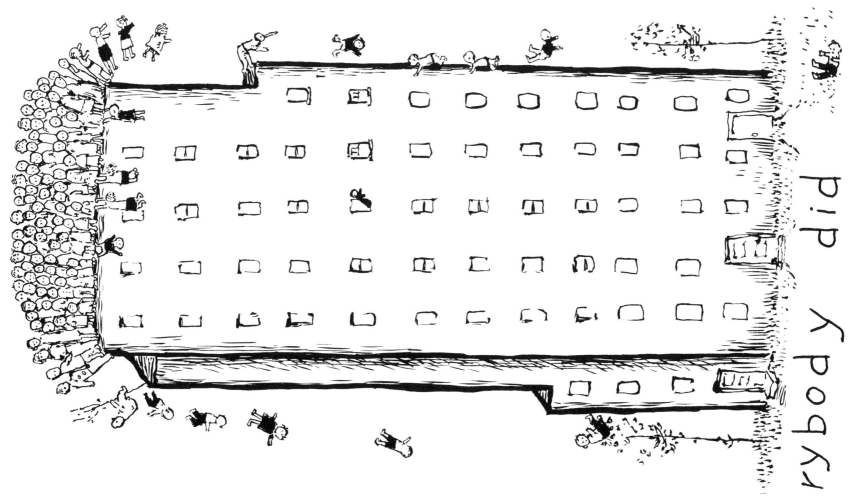

This is what would happen if Eve

Always cry?

This is what would happen if Everybody did

Put toys on the stair?

This is what would happen if Everybody did

hop over the chair ?

This is what would happen if Everybody did

Drop your cup ?

This is what would happen if Everybody did

Stay up ?

This is what would happen if Everybody did

But when there's.....

ONE WHO LEAVES
NO TRACKS......

ONE WHO DOESN'T
USE TACKS......

ONE WHO
SMELLS A BUD....

ONE WHO STEPS
OVER THE MUD.....

ONE WHO SHUTS
THE DOOR......

..ONE WHO
DOESN'T ROAR....

ONE WHO
PATS THE CAT......

ONE WHO PUTS
ON HIS HAT....

ONE WHO DRESSES
DADDY'S FEET......

ONE WHO LIKES HER SEAT...

ONE WHO DOESN'T SMUDGE. . . . .

ONE WHO HAS A LITTLE FUDGE . . . . .

ONE WHO GETS THE SPLASH IN THE GLASS . . . . .

ONE WHO EATS HASH. . . .

ONE WHO DOESN'T CLIMB HIGH. . . . . .

. . . ONE WHO TRIES NOT TO CRY. . . . . .

ONE WHO PEEKS 'ROUND THE CHAIR. . . .

ONE WHO TAKES TOYS OFF THE STAIR . . . . .

ONE WHO SETS DOWN HIS CUP. . . .

ONE WHO DOESN'T STAY UP. . . . .

WHY, THAT'S EVERYBODY!   AND...

THIS IS WHAT WOULD HAPPEN IF EVERYBODY DID